DECADES OF THE 20th AND 21st CENTURIES

The 1990s

Stephen Feinstein

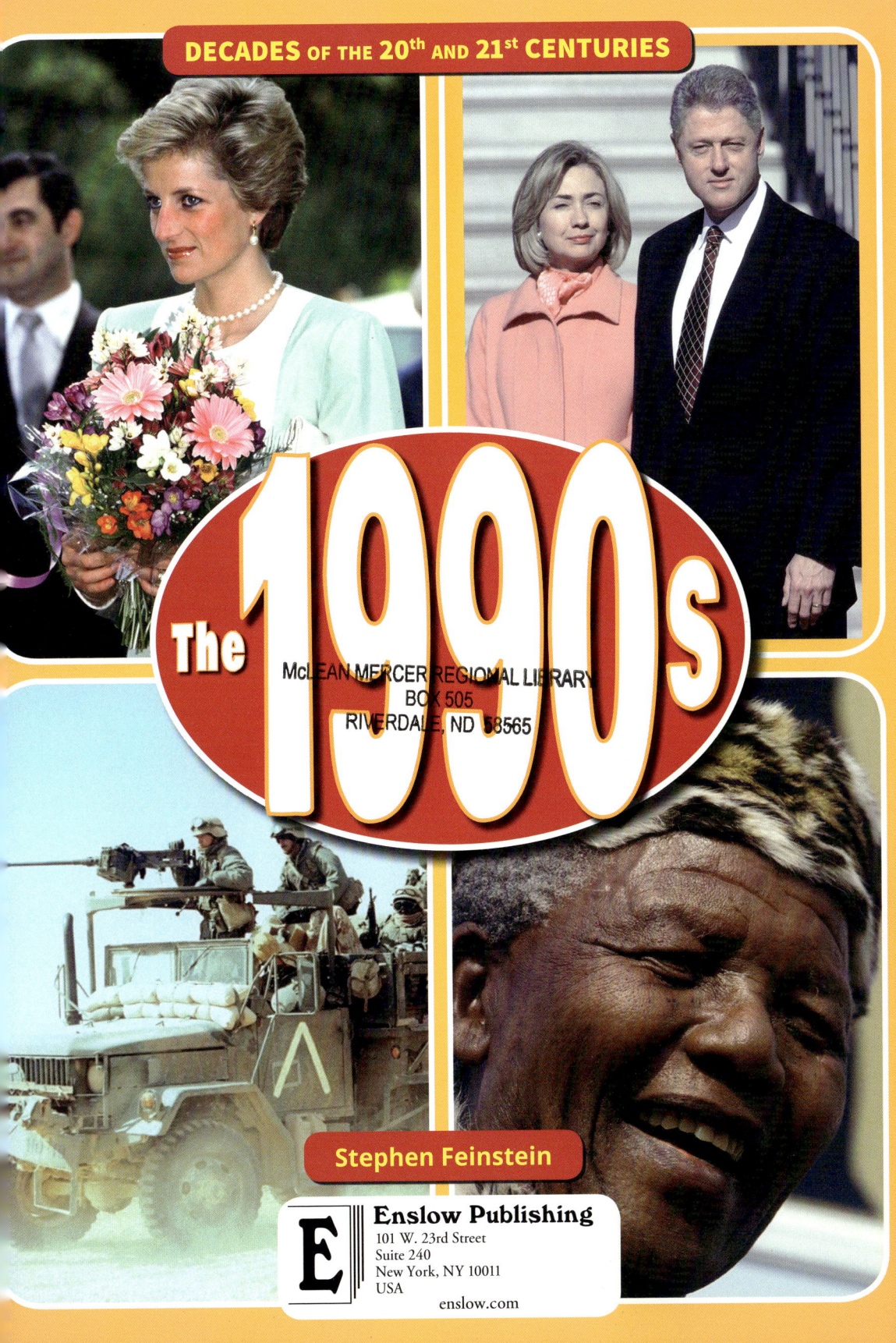

Published in 2016 by Enslow Publishing, LLC.
101 W. 23rd Street, Suite 240, New York, NY 10011

Copyright © 2016 by Enslow Publishing, LLC.
All rights reserved.

No part of this book may be reproduced by any means without the written permission of the publisher.

Library of Congress Cataloging-in-Publication Data

Feinstein, Stephen.
 The 1990s / Stephen Feinstein.
     pages cm. — (Decades of the 20th and 21st centuries)
 Includes bibliographical references and index.
 Summary: "Discusses the decade 1990-1999 in the United States in terms of culture, art, science, and politics"— Provided by publisher.
 Audience: Grade 9 to 12.
 ISBN 978-0-7660-6937-4
 1. United States—Civilization—1945- —Juvenile literature. 2. United States—Politics and government—1989-1993—Juvenile literature. 3. United States—Politics and government—1993-2001—Juvenile literature. 4. Nineteen eighties—Juvenile literature. I. Title.
 E169.12.F4476 2015
 973.929—dc23

2015011322

Printed in the United States of America

To Our Readers: We have done our best to make sure all Web sites in this book were active and appropriate when we went to press. However, the author and the publisher have no control over and assume no liability for the material available on those Web sites or on any Web sites they may link to. Any comments or suggestions can be sent by e-mail to customerservice@enslow.com.

Photo Credits: 7831/Gamma-Rapho via Getty Images, p. 35; Alexis DUCLOS/Gamma-Rapho via Getty Images, p. 61;Augusta National/Masters historic Imagery/Getty Images, p. 40; Brian Brainerd/The Denver Post via Getty Images, p. 36; BOB GALBRAITH/AFP/Getty Images, p. 18, 89 (bottom); Brian Brainerd/ The Denver Post via Getty Images, p. 36; Bryan Yablonsky/Sportschrome/Getty Images, p. 43; Car Culture/ Car Culture ® Collection/Getty Images, p. 83; Cynthia Johnson/The LIFE Images Collection/Getty Images, p. 53; David Brauchli/Hulton Archive/Getty images, p. 63; Eric BOUVET/Gamma-Rapho via Getty Images, p. 49; Frederic REGLAIN/Gamma-Rapho via Getty Images, p. 10; Georges MERILLON/Gamma-Rapho/ Gamma-Keystone via Getty Images, pp. 3 (bottom right), 69, 87 (top); Getty Images Sport/Getty Images, p. 46; Grabowsky/ullstein bild via Getty Images, pp. 70, 88 (top); Herve BRUHAT/Gamma-Rapho via Getty Images, p. 74; Jayne Fincher/Princess Diana Archive/Hulton Royals Collection/Getty Images, pp. 3 (top left), 27; Ken Jarecke/Department Of Defense (DOD)/The LIFE Picture Collection/Getty Images (bottom left); Mick Hutson/Redferns/Getty Images, p. 31; PASCAL GUYOT/AFP/Getty Images, p. 65, 89 (top); Peter Charlesworth/LightRocket via Getty Images, p. 79; Per-Anders Pettersson/Hulton Archive/Getty Images, p 73; PHILIP LITTLETON/AFP/Getty Images, p. 66; Pool BASSIGNAC/STEVENS/Gamma-Rapho via Getty Images, p. 58, 87 (bottom); Rex Rystedt/ The LIFE Images Collection/Getty Images, p. 13; Richard Ellis/Hulton Archive/Getty Images, p. 3 (top right); Robert Giroux/Hulton Archive/Getty Images, pp. 57, 85, 90 (top); Ron Galella/WireImage/Ron Galella Collection/Getty images, p. 39, 44, 88 (bottom); Ron Galella, Ltd./WireImage/Ron Galella Collection/Getty Images, p. 29; Science & Society Picture Library/SSPL/Getty Images, pp. 6, 77, 80, 90 (bottom); Serge Attal/The LIFE Images Collection/Getty Images, p. 16; Steve Grayson/WireImage/ Getty Images, p. 20; Time Life Pictures/Fbi/The LIFE Picture Collection/Getty Images, p. 54; Tim Roney/ Hulton Archive/Getty Images, p. 32; Tyler Hicks/Hulton Archive/Getty Images, p. 62; VINCE BUCCI/AFP/ Getty Images, p. 23; Visions of America/UIG via Getty Images, p. 50; Wendy Maeda/The Boston Globe via Getty Images, p.14; Yvonne Hemsey/Hulton Archive/Getty Images, p. 24.

Cover Credits: Georges MERILLON/Gamma-Rapho/Gamma-Keystone via Getty Images (Nelson Mandela); Jayne Fincher/Princess Diana Archive/Hulton Royals Collection/Getty Images (Diana); Ken Jarecke/ Department Of Defense (DOD)/The LIFE Picture Collection/Getty Images (soldiers); Richard Ellis/Hulton Archive/Getty Images (Bill and Hillary Clinton).

Contents

Introduction 7

Pop Culture, Lifestyles, and Fashion 9

Entertainment and the Arts 28

Sports 41

National and International Politics 48

Advances in Science, Technology, and Medicine 75

Conclusion 84

    Timeline 87

    Glossary 91

    Further Reading 92

    Index 94

The development of the Internet radically changed society.

Introduction

The 1990s began on an optimistic note. The Berlin Wall had just been torn down late in 1989, which brought a symbolic end to the forty-five-year-long Cold War between the United States and the Soviet Union. After the fall of the wall, the communist governments of Eastern Europe fell, too, one by one. In 1991, the Soviet Union itself collapsed. Russians then began the difficult process of changing their nation into a democratic society. Now that the Cold War was over, Americans could look forward to peace. But the world would not be a peaceful place in the 1990s. The United States would take on the task of policing the world as the only superpower.

In spite of these problems, the 1990s proved to be a period of prosperity for many Americans. The United States had its greatest boom economy in post–World War II history. Perhaps the biggest changes in the economy and society came about through the development of the Internet.

This global computer network quickly became part of everyday life. E-mail, web browsers, and search engines were powerful new tools. They made it easy to find information and talk with others. Students did research online. Shoppers bought items from home instead of going to a store. People could make new friends in faraway places. The Internet changed society.

New technology could not solve all of the world's problems, however. In some cases, it added to them. The Internet enabled thieves to commit crimes online. People debated the potential risks of cloning animals. As the decade closed, people worried that a potential computer glitch called Y2K might bring disaster to our technology-driven society.

By the 1990s, computers were the gateway to important new discoveries. With computers, scientists studied the blueprints of life. They began the Human Genome Project in 1990. This was a massive effort to learn how the human body grows and develops. A few years later, scientists discovered a way to clone animals. They made an exact copy of a sheep. New technology also aided the study of space. In 1990, the Hubble Space Telescope was launched into orbit. It offered amazing views of the universe. In 1997, a tiny rover roamed the surface of Mars. It sent back stunning images of the Red Planet.

Some of humanity's most ancient problems also remained. Medicine had made great strides, but fatal illnesses still existed. The deadly disease HIV/AIDS ravaged Africa during the 1990s. Conflicts still plagued the world, as well. In the Middle East, Iraq invaded Kuwait during the summer of 1990. Troops from across the globe united to free the tiny kingdom in early 1991. Later in the decade, a new group of terrorists gained strength. Their organization, known as al-Qaeda, began a war of terror against the United States and its allies.

Foreign terrorists were not the only threat. In 1995, a US citizen blew up a government building in Oklahoma. Four years later, two high school students went on a deadly rampage in Colorado. They killed thirteen classmates and teachers before taking their own lives. Even larger massacres were taking place in other parts of the world. In Bosnia and Rwanda, enormous groups of people were killed because of ethnic differences.

As the final decade of the twentieth century ended, people looked to the future. Technology promised more great discoveries, yet it also promised more challenges. It rushed the pace of life. It made families and friends more isolated from each other. The 1990s showed that technology had benefits and drawbacks.

Pop Culture, Lifestyles, and Fashion

Today it is hard to imagine life without the Internet. The vast network connects computers from all across the globe. We use it for work, for entertainment, and to talk with others. Yet the Internet is a relatively new invention. It only became widely available in the mid-1990s.

The Rise of the Internet

During the 1990s, the Internet brought a whole new world right to people's fingertips. It was the world of cyberspace, which was often called the information superhighway. In an instant, anyone with access to a computer, modem, and telephone line could connect to huge databases anywhere in the world. With a few simple clicks of a mouse, powerful search engines would retrieve information from the World Wide Web. Scientists and engineers worked constantly to find ways to make information pass faster over the Internet.

Online, a person could read magazines, news articles, encyclopedia entries, even entire books. Such information was available at any time day or night. Before long, some people felt they were drowning in information.

Of course, having so much information available did not necessarily mean it was all accurate or good. Easy access to the Internet meant

that almost anyone—even those with faulty information or dangerous motives—could post sites for the public to view.

New and Different Ways to Communicate

The Internet brought a new way to communicate with people. E-mail was easy. Often it was more convenient and cheaper than using the telephone. A person could send an e-mail message at any time of day or night without fear of disturbing the recipient, who could respond when it was convenient.

Another Internet function that became extremely popular was the chat room. People could have ongoing discussions with all kinds of people. Since the true identity of participants was usually unknown, many people invented their own online personalities and identified themselves by a code word. Although this secrecy helped protect Internet users' privacy, it also led to new dangers. Now criminals could approach their victims and win their trust under a fake name.

Many hailed the Internet for its great success in easing communication. Advocates claimed the Internet was bringing Americans closer together. Yet, more and more Americans were suddenly spending countless hours alone staring at their computer screens. It was often said that the Internet simultaneously brought people together and kept them apart.

Buying and Selling Online

By the end of 1999, more than forty million American households were on the Internet. Large numbers of people had begun shopping online. Amazon.com was the largest online retailer to emerge during the 1990s. Jeff Bezos, the founder of Amazon.com, started by selling books online. As Amazon's name became more widely known, Bezos began offering music CDs and videos. Later, Amazon began selling toys. Teaming up with other companies, Amazon was soon selling everything from lawn mowers to pet supplies to prescription drugs. By decade's end, however, Amazon.com had yet to earn a dime in profit. Only time would tell if such an Internet business model, which carried enormous costs for startup and advertising, would work.

The Internet made possible new ways of buying and selling. A company called eBay began to host online auctions. Another company, Priceline.com, allowed people to bargain for the best prices on items such as airline tickets, hotel room reservations, and groceries. Soon, traditional companies began to move onto the Internet. A growing number of Americans even began doing their banking and paying their bills online.

As more Americans logged on to the Internet, some people worried that records of a person's net surfing and shopping habits could be viewed by organizations such as online advertising agencies and marketing companies. Online privacy became a controversial issue by the end of the decade, especially because of the fear that thieves could get access to credit card numbers and use the information to destroy someone's financial standing.

Internet Boom

Thousands of people took the Internet craze a step further and started their own businesses on the Web. A new career was created. Known as Webmasters, these people knew how to design, create, and maintain Web sites. Inspired by new Internet businesses, such as Amazon.com, people frantically tried to borrow money for their businesses. Many raised huge sums. Quite a few Internet companies eventually sold stock to eager investors.

Before long, the media was full of stories about the new dot-com millionaires. Many of them were young men and women in their twenties. By the end of the decade, however, very few of these new

Jeff Bezos founded e-commerce giant Amazon.com in 1994.

The Road to the Information Superhighway

Scientists working for the US Department of Defense began building a computer network in the late 1960s. They needed to work together across long distances. The scientists found a way to link their computers. They swapped data via telephone lines and cables. At first, the public had little access to the network, which was called ARPANET (Advanced Research Projects Agency Network). However, during the 1980s, growing numbers of people began purchasing personal computers. Some began connecting to ARPANET through what were called bulletin-board systems, or BBSs.

In 1989, a British scientist named Timothy Berners-Lee invented the World Wide Web. It added pictures and sound to the text-only Internet. Using Berners-Lee's system, users could perform a search and click on links to visit other sites. By 1993, programs called browsers were making the Web easily accessible to everyone. Before long, millions of people were going online. They hailed the Internet as the information superhighway.

companies were making profits. They were spending lavishly on marketing, and cash reserves were beginning to dwindle. It seemed that the boom of Internet business could not last forever, and that a reversal of fortune would soon occur.

Cellular Phones

Toward the end of the 1990s, the use of cellular telephones rose dramatically. An increasingly common sight on city streets was a person walking along while chatting into a cell phone held up to his or her ear. It often seemed as though people were talking to themselves and oblivious to the fact that other people could not help but overhear their conversations.

Unfortunately, more Americans were also carrying on phone conversations while driving. Because this habit was dangerous and caused frequent accidents, some towns passed laws against using cell phones while driving.

Bomb Explodes in the World Trade Center

The twin towers of the World Trade Center dominated New York City's skyline. The tallest buildings in the city, they were a symbol of America's business strength. In 1993, terrorists tried to destroy the towers with a bomb.

In February 1993, Muslim terrorists set off a car bomb at the World Trade Center in New York City. The terrorists had hoped to topple the buildings, but their bomb was not strong enough. The attack did, however, kill six people and injure more than a thousand.

The men involved in the bombing were later caught. They had links to al-Qaeda, a terrorist group from the Middle East. In 1993, few people had heard of al-Qaeda. Less than a decade later, everyone would know about the terrorist organization. The group had declared war on the United States. The World Trade Center bombing of 1993

Seeing people talk on cell phones was still a strange sight in the '90s.

was the first time al-Qaeda was involved in a large attack against a US target. In the years ahead, al-Qaeda would strike many more times. The attacks would grow ever more deadly. On September 11, 2001, al-Qaeda achieved its goal of destroying the twin towers when terrorists flew airplanes into the buildings.

Terror Bombing in Oklahoma City

Another unbelievable episode occurred on April 19, 1995, when Timothy McVeigh, a decorated Army veteran with ties to right-wing militia organizations, used a powerful truck bomb to blow up the Alfred P. Murrah Federal Building in Oklahoma City, Oklahoma. The bombing killed 168 men, women, and children and injured hundreds more.

Americans were shocked to learn that a US citizen had set the bomb. McVeigh was a disenfranchised loner who believed that the US government robbed people of their freedom. His act of terrorism was a sort of revenge on what he believed was a tyrannical government. McVeigh was caught soon after the bombing. He was convicted and was executed for his crime in 2001. Terry Nichols, a friend who had helped McVeigh build the bomb, was also convicted. Nichols was sent to prison for life.

School Shooting at Columbine

The behavior of terrorists is hard to understand. Even harder to understand were several shootings that occurred in American public schools. Within a two-year period, there were five mass school shootings in the United States.

The worst incident occurred at Columbine High School in Littleton, Colorado, on April 20, 1999. Two students, Dylan Klebold and Eric Harris, burst into the school and shot at students and teachers. They also threw pipe bombs. Their rampage lasted more than

The Unabomber

Harvard graduate and former mathematics professor Ted Kaczynski found himself wandering around from city to city, never quite connecting with society. Distrustful of technology and its progression, Kaczynski moved to a plot of land in Montana and began living off the grid. There, he started work on his Unabomber Manifesto.

In 1978 Kaczynski sent a letter bomb to a professor. The bomb injured a police officer. This would be the first of sixteen letter bombs that Kaczynski would send over the years, primarily to universities and airlines. Authorities could not find Kaczynski because the letter bombs detonated and left no evidence.

Finally, Kaczynski reached out to the press anonymously, hoping to have his manifesto published. Eager to end the bombing campaign as he had promised, the *New York Times* and *Washington Post* each ran portions of Kaczynski's manuscript. His brother recognized the writing and turned Ted Kaczynski in. Kaczynski was arrested in 1996, and was sentenced to life in prison. He had managed to kill three people and injure twenty-nine others before his capture.

forty-five minutes. As police closed in, the attackers committed suicide. They killed twelve students and a teacher before killing themselves. The two young killers had belonged to a group whose members wore long black trench coats and called themselves the Trench Coat Mafia.

Investigators learned that the young men had a dark history. They had been arrested for theft. Violent video games, films, and music fascinated them. At school, they had been bullied. They resented athletes and popular students. Many observers believed Klebold and Harris were so alienated or so emotionally immature that they could not distinguish between the real world and the virtual reality of computer games. Or perhaps the two just wanted to make a name for themselves.

After the shootings at Columbine, the safety and well-being of the nation's schoolchildren suddenly seemed to be at great risk. It was clear that a lot more attention needed to be paid to any teenager who seemed to be having emotional problems. Some places also took steps—such as installing metal detectors and carrying out locker searches—to keep dangerous weapons out of schools.

Race Riots Rock Los Angeles

In 1992, a huge riot rocked the city of Los Angeles. The rioters destroyed homes and businesses, causing more than a billion dollars in damage. A court case sparked the Los Angeles riot. Four white police officers were on trial for beating Rodney King, a black suspect, when he resisted arrest for a traffic violation. The police officers shot him twice with an electric stun gun. They punched and kicked him, and they kept hitting King even after he was on the ground. A witness captured part of the incident on videotape. The video aired on TV all across the country.

In April 1992, a jury made up of ten whites, one Hispanic, and one Asian found the police officers not guilty. African American and Latino

Soldiers were called to control the riots sparked by the King verdict.

residents of Los Angeles were furious. Thousands stormed the streets. They attacked innocent bystanders, started fires, and looted stores. Street gangs added to the mayhem. The rioting lasted for almost a week. Finally, soldiers helped police halt the violence.

Nearly five thousand buildings were destroyed or badly damaged in the riots. More than fifty people died during the rioting in Los Angeles. Another twenty-three hundred were seriously injured. Some of the rioters who broke laws were later arrested, but many avoided punishment. In 1993, the four police officers involved in the beating of Rodney King were again put on trial. This time they were charged with the federal crime of violating King's civil rights. Two of the officers were acquitted. The other two were found guilty. They were sentenced to prison terms of two and a half years.

O.J. Simpson Murder Trial

The most glaring example of America's racial divide was the opposing responses of blacks and whites to the O. J. Simpson trial. African-American football hero and movie actor O. J. Simpson was accused of murdering his former wife, Nicole Brown, and her friend Ron Goldman, both of whom were white. The two had been found gruesomely stabbed to death in June 1994. Though he claimed his innocence, Simpson was arrested and brought to trial. The whole nation became almost obsessed with the trial. There was unprecedented daily television coverage, and many Americans remained glued to their televisions, as if they were watching a soap opera.

Much circumstantial evidence seemed to point to Simpson's guilt, especially DNA evidence. But Simpson's attorneys portrayed their client as a victim of a racist white justice system. They accused the Los Angeles Police Department (the same police force that had been involved in the Rodney King beating) of racial bias. They said LAPD officers had planted evidence to frame Simpson. The jury found

Simpson not guilty. In a startling contrast, 85 percent of African Americans agreed with the verdict while only 32 percent of whites did. The case showed not only the racial tensions in America but economic problems, as well. Simpson was a wealthy man who could afford world-class attorneys. Many believed he was able to buy his way out of trouble. However, a later civil trial found him responsible for the deaths of his ex-wife and Ron Goldman and forced him to pay huge sums in damages.

1990s Fashion

During the 1990s, many fashions were recycled from previous decades. The grunge look that began in the late 1980s was still popular with teens, while some rappers and hip-hoppers continued to wear oversized clothes with pants hanging low around their hips. Pierced eyebrows, noses, and other body parts were popular, as were ragged jeans with holes in them. Tattoos on various parts of the body were more popular than ever. Even retro items, such as miniskirts and bell-bottoms, could often be seen.

In the business world, more people were dressing casually. The trend had started with casual Fridays, which was the one day of the week on which many companies allowed employees to come to work without their usual formal business suit. Perhaps the new casual attitude had something to do with the dot-com companies, where it was hard to find an employee over the age of thirty. But increasingly, in dot-com companies, as well as in some older companies, casual Fridays were being extended to every day of the week. Increasingly, the same outfits were appropriate for both work and play.

Beanie Babies and Furbies

Throughout the 1990s, several fads erupted that would rival the hysteria caused by novelties of earlier decades, such as the pet rock

O.J. Simpson famously tried on gloves that did not fit during his trial.

The robotic toy Furby was in demand during the 1998 holidays.

of the 1970s or the Cabbage Patch Kids of the 1980s. Most of these fads were children's toys, and they made both parents and children embark on mad searches to find the newest and rarest items.

Among the most popular toys of the 1990s were Beanie Babies, which were small animals filled with bean-bag stuffing. Beanies came in all shapes, sizes, and colors, and they were marketed as collector's items. Many American households owned dozens—if not hundreds—of the Beanies. Finding new—or better yet, rare or retired—pieces was all the rage. Fast-food chains got in on the action, too, giving away miniature Beanies with children's meals. These promotions often caused long lines and rapid sell outs. Some companies even began to produce Beanie-related merchandise, such as storage bags or special shelves to hold the valuable Beanie collections.

Other toy fads included the Furby, which is a furry, though not quite identifiable, creature specially equipped with electronics that enabled it to speak, move, and perform other pet-like functions. Children all over America became almost obsessed with "feeding" or otherwise caring for their Furbies. Some teachers found the toys so distracting that they were forced to confiscate them—at least until the end of the school day.

Princess Diana Dies

One of the most tragic events of the 1990s happened on August 31, 1997. England's Princess Diana, who had only a year earlier been divorced from Charles, the Prince of Wales, was killed in a car crash in Paris, France. Known as the People's Princess, Diana had long been a symbol of glamour and style, but she was also well known for her work with many different charities. Despite her break with the British royal family, Diana was seen as a caring, affectionate mother and a great humanitarian who had lent a touch of charm to British royalty. Coverage of Diana's funeral and moving tributes to her life had people glued to their televisions the world over.

Americans were shaken when Princess Diana was killed in a car accident.

Entertainment and the Arts

While there was still room for popular music and blockbuster movies in the 1990s, the decade was rife with alternative offerings. Suddenly, art house movies and music played on college radio stations were bursting into the mainstream. Quirkiness was cool, and a show about nothing ruled TV.

Musical Variety

Like fashion, musical styles from previous decades refused to go away in the 1990s. Every possible variety of music attracted its own following. The sophisticated lyrical harmonies of groups such as Boyz II Men and 'N Sync were popular with music lovers who sought beauty and sweetness in their music, as well as with young girls who considered the male vocalists heartthrobs. Equally popular were hip-hop and gangsta rap, which appealed to fans who liked the anguished cries of the city street being set to rhythm. Superstars from earlier decades, such as Sting and the Rolling Stones, also remained popular with older people and with young people to whom they were a fresh new sound.

Boyz II Men wowed listeners with their emotional harmonies.

Many young people were searching for a musical style to call their own. In the early years of the decade, some found it in the music of Kurt Cobain and his band, Nirvana. Cobain's music cried out for a rejection of all that was bland and slick in American culture, including the prevailing styles of pop music. Young people responded to Nirvana's rebellious spirit. The music, characterized by loud guitar distortion, became known as grunge music. Alternative music as a genre had been around for a while and often played on college radio stations. In the 1990s it crossed over into the mainstream thanks to the popularity of bands such as Nirvana.

The Internet Changes the Music Industry

The term alternative was applied to so many different artists and groups that it eventually became meaningless. In one sense, however, it pointed to new developments. The growth of the Internet made possible a whole new way of producing and distributing music, as well as listening to it. Small independent, or indie, labels had managed to produce albums over the years with varying degrees of success in the shadow of the major music companies. Now with the Internet, it became possible for anyone to become an independent producer. A musician could put his or her own music on the Web, and anyone with access to the Internet could easily download the music. Thus was born a true alternative to the major labels. By the end of the decade, the big recording companies were grappling with the issue of music piracy, as previously copyrighted music became available to download for free.

One company called Napster let its users swap their music at no cost over the Internet. Any recorded song was available for free to Napster's twenty million users. The major labels, alarmed at the prospect of losing enormous sums of money, took legal action against Napster and other companies.

Grunge and Hip Hop

A wide variety of music was played in the 1990s, but two genres—grunge and hip-hop—stood out as not just styles of music but as entire cultures. Grunge evolved from punk music and heavy metal. Hip-hop grew out of the rap music of the 1980s.

Grunge music started in Seattle, Washington. The bands Nirvana and Pearl Jam came from this city. So did Soundgarden and Alice in Chains. These groups created a unique sound using heavy guitar riffs and dark, gloomy lyrics. Grunge fans did not want to be flashy. They dressed in flannel shirts and ripped jeans. In 1994, Nirvana singer and grunge poster boy Kurt Cobain (pictured) killed himself. In the years afterward, the popularity of grunge music began to decline.

Hip-hop moved in two directions during the 1990s. Gangsta rap stressed the violent side of city life. Artists rapped about street gangs, drive-by shootings, and police brutality. Ice Cube and Ice-T were two early gangsta rappers. Other hip-hop artists rejected gangsta culture. Performers, such as Will Smith and LL Cool J, scored hits with more upbeat themes. Hip-hop fans of the 1990s liked baggy jeans and sports jerseys. They wore their baseball caps sideways. Unlike grunge, hip-hop music and culture remains popular today.

Christina Aguilera hit the pop music scene with a powerful voice.

Edgar Bronfman Jr., head of Universal, the world's biggest music company, said that soon "a few clicks of your mouse will make it possible for you to summon every book ever written in any language, every movie ever made, every television show ever produced, and every piece of music ever recorded." Clearly, the major music labels—as well as book publishers and other corporations—would have to find a way to function alongside the expanding Internet.

Popularity of Latin Music

Following in the footsteps of Cuban-American singing sensation Gloria Estefan and Panamanian-born singer Rubén Blades, Latino musicians traveled the crossover route in the 1990s by recording music that appealed to both Hispanic and non-Hispanic Americans. Their flashy videos featured the fancy footwork of sensual dancers. Singer Ricky Martin thrilled millions of fans with his passionate endorsement of a wild and crazy lifestyle. Singers Marc Anthony and Christina Aguilera also attracted a wide following.

Probably one of the most amazing musical developments involved a group of elderly Cuban musicians who had performed at the Buena Vista Social Club in Havana about fifty years earlier. American guitarist Ry Cooder, an avid fan of Cuban music, visited the island to record and jam with Cuban musicians. He located some of the Buena Vista musicians who were living in poverty and obscurity, not having performed for many years. Seventy-two-year-old lead singer Ibrahim Ferrer, for example, now shined shoes for a living. Cooder brought the musicians together, organized recording sessions, and produced an album and a movie about the musicians and their music. The project was successful beyond anyone's wildest dreams. It resulted in worldwide fame for the musicians of the Buena Vista Social Club and concerts in places such as New York's Carnegie Hall.

The Magic of *Harry Potter*

In 1997, a new book thrilled young readers. Author J. K. Rowling wrote the story of a young wizard named Harry Potter, who attended the Hogwarts School of Witchcraft and Wizardry. Before long, people all over the world were reading about Harry's adventures.

Rowling had begun writing stories at age six. However, she did not find success as a writer until she was thirty-two years old. In the mid-1990s, Rowling was unemployed and raising a small child on her own. Yet she refused to give up on her writing. Rowling had an idea for a book about a boy wizard. She wrote the first *Harry Potter* novel in cafés while her daughter slept beside her.

Harry Potter and the Sorcerer's Stone was one of the best-selling novels of all time. The story charmed readers of all ages. They enjoyed the magical world of Harry and his friends. J. K. Rowling wrote six more *Harry Potter* books, which became best sellers, as well as Hollywood movies.

The *Harry Potter* books have sold more than five hundred million copies. They have been printed in sixty-seven languages. Today, the *Harry Potter* series still enchants readers, and J.K. Rowling is an extremely wealthy celebrity.

At the Movies

Like everything else in the 1990s, moviemaking made extensive use of cutting-edge computer technology and new digitalization techniques. In 1993, director Steven Spielberg produced *Jurassic Park*. It became an instant hit with moviegoers who were thrilled by the dinosaurs thundering across the screen. The prehistoric creatures were so startlingly real that it was hard to believe actual dinosaurs had not been captured on film.

Taking technology a step further, *Toy Story* (1996) was the first feature-length animated film created entirely by computer. It

Kids and adults alike became enchanted with the wizard Harry Potter.

New Ways to Be Entertained

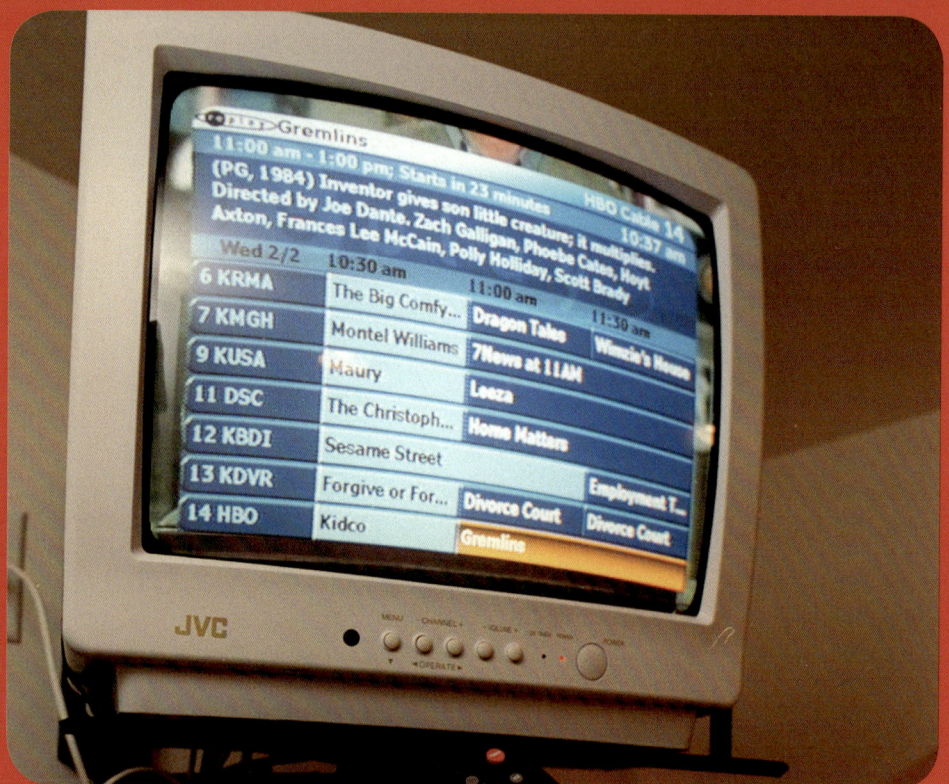

In 1999, TV viewers had a new way to watch their favorite shows. That year, The TiVo company introduced a home version of the digital video recorder (DVR). Using this device, a viewer can pause a program and resume it later without missing any part of it. One popular feature allows the viewer to watch a show commercial-free.

TV viewers who enjoyed watching movies at home by either renting or buying videocassettes also had a new way to enjoy movies. In 1997, DVDs became widely available. DVDs had superior sound and image quality as compared to videocassettes.

revolutionized the art of animation. Similar films soon followed, including *Antz* and *A Bug's Life*.

In music videos and some films, a technique called morphing made it possible to manipulate images of people in new ways. One person could even be transformed into another.

Computer technology was also used in the movie *Titanic* to convince audiences that the huge ocean liner they saw disappear beneath the waves on screen was the real ship *Titanic*. This disaster film became one of the biggest movie hits of all time.

Though he excelled at creating technologically advanced hits, Steven Spielberg also produced some great dramatic films during the 1990s. *Schindler's List* (1993) was a drama portraying the heroic deeds of Oskar Schindler, a German industrialist who rescued Jews employed at his factory from death during the Holocaust. In 1998, Spielberg produced the World War II drama *Saving Private Ryan*. It included an amazingly realistic depiction of the sheer terror experienced by American soldiers as they stormed ashore on the beaches of Normandy, France, during the D-Day invasion of Europe.

Era of the Sitcom

One of the strangest developments in entertainment during the 1990s was the popularity of so-called shows about nothing. Steering away from traditional sitcoms (situational comedies) with off-the-wall plots, some new television programs began to try to depict characters with problems and interests like those of real people. Three of the most popular sitcoms of the 1990s were *Seinfeld*, *Friends*, and *The Simpsons*.

Seinfeld was based on the real-life observations of comedian Jerry Seinfeld. Each week, Jerry and his three friends dealt with everyday problems that viewers found humorous. Many scenes took place in

Jerry's tiny apartment. Viewers enjoyed the show's witty jokes and clever plots. *Seinfeld* ran for nine seasons before finishing in 1998.

Friends first aired in 1994. The show was about six young men and women trying to succeed in New York City. *Friends* was an instant hit. Young adult viewers identified with the group's amusing dilemmas. The six cast members became celebrities. They went on to star in movies and other TV shows. More than fifty million people watched the final episode of *Friends* in 2004.

The Simpsons is the longest running sitcom ever. Although it began as short sketches, the half-hour version of the show debuted in 1990. At the time, the idea of an animated sitcom was unique. However, the Simpson family became part of American culture. Their antics kept viewers laughing through the 1990s and beyond.

Seinfeld *ran for most of the 1990s and is still aired in reruns today.*

Tiger Woods's youth and talent brought a new popularity to golf.

Sports

By the 1990s, basketball and football were catching up with baseball in popularity. New records would be broken and new sports would be pursued as the emergence of alternative sports stayed true to the theme of this decade.

Tiger Woods Changes Golf

In previous decades, golf appealed mainly to rich people. Typical golfers were businessmen trying to maintain good relationships with colleagues and clients. During the 1990s, some 3.2 million new golfers—mostly younger men and women in their twenties and thirties—took up the sport.

One person who was responsible for the sudden increased popularity of golf was the amazing young professional golf champion Eldrick "Tiger" Woods. In 1991, Woods became the youngest winner of the United States Junior Amateur championship. He captured that title again in 1992 and 1993. He went professional in 1996 and won two Professional Golf Association (PGA) titles that year and was named the PGA Tour's outstanding rookie. As Woods's popularity grew, more new golfers rushed to try their own hand at the sport. Fans admired Woods's incredibly powerful long shots, as well as his expert putting.

In 1997, Woods became the first African American golfer to win the Masters Tournament. He shot a record 270 over 72 holes and finished 12 strokes ahead of the rest of the players. In 1999, he won eight PGA tournaments in one year and became the first golfer in more than two decades to do so. During the 1999–2000 season, Woods earned more than $6 million in prize money for his winning streak of six consecutive victories. The champion golfer was now a rich man, although partly thanks to his fame, golf was no longer just a rich man's sport.

Baseball's Ups and Downs

In August 1994, major-league baseball players went on a strike that lasted until the following spring. Not only were baseball fans deprived of the last part of the 1994 baseball season, but the strike also caused the cancellation of the World Series. Fans were outraged. When the 1995 baseball season started late, many angry fans stayed away from the games. Baseball stands stood nearly empty throughout the 1995 season.

Slowly, though, fans went back. Americans loved baseball too much to hold a grudge forever. And a few emerging champions were causing excitement. In 1996, the Baltimore Orioles' "Iron Man" shortstop Cal Ripken Jr. broke Lou Gehrig's record of playing in 2,130 straight games. From 1982 through 1996, Ripken played in 2,216 consecutive games. Fans grew even more excited during the 1998 season when not one but two ballplayers broke Roger Maris's 1961 record of 61 home runs in one season. Mark McGwire of the St. Louis Cardinals hit 70 homers, and Sammy Sosa of the Chicago Cubs hit 66. Unfortunately, allegations of steroid use in later years would cast doubt on the legitimacy of these home run records.

Cal Ripken Jr. broke Gehrig's consecutive games record in 1996.

HIV/AIDS in Sports

In the early 1990s, Americans were just beginning to realize how many people were infected with HIV, the virus that causes AIDS. Several famous athletes revealed that they had the disease. Among them were Arthur Ashe, Magic Johnson, and Greg Louganis.

Arthur Ashe (*pictured*) was the first African American man to win a major tennis title. During his career, he won many events, including Wimbledon and the US Open. Ashe probably became infected with HIV when he received tainted blood during heart surgery. In 1992, he revealed that he had AIDS. Ashe spoke publicly about the plight of people suffering from AIDS until he died in 1993 at age forty-nine.

Earvin "Magic" Johnson was one of the NBA's greatest players. During the 1980s, he led the Los Angeles Lakers to five championship titles. In 1991, the thirty-two-year-old Johnson learned that he had HIV. He retired from basketball but briefly returned later. Johnson went on to become an activist for HIV/AIDS awareness.

Greg Louganis had studied dance and gymnastics before turning his talents to diving. At the 1984 Olympics, Louganis won two gold medals for diving. He repeated this feat at the 1988 Olympics. In 1994, Louganis announced that he is gay, and the following year he revealed he had tested positive for HIV in 1988. Almost immediately, corporate sponsors dropped his endorsements. The stigma of HIV/AIDS was very real.

Olympic Bombing

An incident at the 1996 Summer Olympics reminded Americans, who were still shaken by the 1995 Oklahoma City bombing, of the danger of terrorism. Atlanta, Georgia, had been selected to host the Summer Games. No expense was spared to put on the most extravagant Games in the history of the Olympics.

Huge crowds flocked to Atlanta. Unfortunately, among them was someone who was up to no good. A pipe bomb exploded in Olympic Park and killed two people. Earlier, a security guard named Richard Jewel had found and reported a mysteriously abandoned backpack. He was arrested and wrongly accused of the bombing. After a long investigation, he was released. The true bomber has never been found, although federal authorities continue to pursue possible suspects. Unfortunately, the violent incident overshadowed the Olympic Games themselves, during which the United States won a total of 101 medals, 44 of them gold.

Extreme Sports

During the 1990s, a growing number of American athletes were drawn to challenging kinds of activities called extreme sports. Not content to ski down slopes that were considered difficult by most skiers, for example, extreme skiers skied down vertical cliffs and sometimes dropped considerable distances in free fall before landing on the snowy slopes below. Such skiing seemed to be thrilling—for those who survived!

Another extreme sport was long-distance rowing. Tori Murden, a thirty-six-year-old Kentucky lawyer, is a member of the Sector No Limits Team. This group of athletes is dedicated to testing the limits of human endurance. Not content to row across a lake or river, Murden set her sights on the Atlantic Ocean. Murden proved to be perhaps the most persistent rower of all time. She had tried and failed to row

X Games

The alternative culture of the 1990s extended into sports. During this time, Generation Xers who were into grunge and an alternative lifestyle enjoyed snowboarding, skateboarding, and motocross.

In 1995, the sports channel ESPN launched the first X Games, which is a sort of Olympics for extreme sports. That year, some of the events were roller blading, mountain biking, street luging, and bungee jumping. Approximately two hundred thousand fans flocked to Newport, Rhode Island to watch the games. People responded to the casual feel of the event, not to mention the exciting, death-defying antics of the daredevil athletes.

The X Games proved so popular that a winter games were added. The X Games are held annually in January and August in the United States, and separate X Games are held in Europe and Asia.

across the Atlantic twice in 1998. Her boat capsized fifteen times during Hurricane Danielle, and she had to be rescued. Finally, in 1999, she became the first American—and the first woman—to row three thousand miles across the Atlantic Ocean. She survived being tossed into the sea during Hurricane Lenny when twenty-foot waves caused her twenty-three-foot-long boat, *American Pearl*, to stand on end. Throughout the voyage, Murden avoided loneliness by using a satellite phone to speak to friends and to send email messages to schoolchildren.

National and International Politics

For much of the 1990s, the White House was occupied by President Bill Clinton. The Democrat's term was bookended by two Republican presidents named Bush. Both would lead the country to war. The first was George H.W. Bush, who had served as vice president to Ronald Reagan for most of the 1980s before being elected to his own term in the Oval Office.

Persian Gulf War

In August 1990, Iraq's dictator Saddam Hussein invaded and occupied the country of Kuwait and asserted historical Iraqi claims to that land. Hussein's plan was to gain control of more of the Middle East's oil resources, which would help Iraq's economy. Once it controlled Kuwait, Iraq was a threat to Saudi Arabia, the region's major oil producer and an ally of the United States. George Bush, America's Republican president, had a background as an oil industry executive. He understood very well the importance of oil to America's economy. Bush declared, "This aggression will not stand."

Besides threatening oil supplies, Hussein was known to be developing weapons of mass destruction—nuclear, chemical, and perhaps biological weapons. Comparing Saddam Hussein to Adolf Hitler,

In August 1990, the United States sent troops to protect Saudi Arabia from Iraq.

President George H.W. Bush took an aggressive stand against Iraq.

President Bush assembled a coalition of thirty nations, including many Middle Eastern nations, and began Operation Desert Shield, a massive military buildup in the region and defense of Saudi Arabia. The United Nations immediately sent at least two hundred fifty thousand troops under the command of American General Norman Schwarzkopf. Within several months, that number had grown to more than half a million troops, mostly from the United States.

Once Saudi Arabia was safe, the coalition looked to free Kuwait. Before attacking, the coalition gave Iraq a chance to leave Kuwait peacefully. Saddam Hussein refused. Operation Desert Storm began on January 16, 1991, when the United States and its allies began a campaign of air strikes against Iraq. Television viewers worldwide watched the bombardment of Baghdad, Iraq. Mindful of Americans' bitter memories of the nation's humiliating defeat in the Vietnam War and of all those who had died in vain during the 1960s and early 1970s, General Colin Powell and America's other military leaders in the Persian Gulf War, as Desert Storm came to be called, were determined to keep American casualties to a minimum.

After more than a month of bombings in which many innocent Iraqi civilians died, General Schwarzkopf began a ground invasion of Iraq on February 23. Within just one hundred hours, the Persian Gulf War was over. More than one hundred fifty thousand Iraqi soldiers and civilians were killed, along with 141 American soldiers. Kuwait had been liberated from Iraqi control. The threat to Middle East oil had been eliminated, although Iraqi forces set fire to Kuwait's oil fields as they fled the country. Saddam Hussein was allowed to remain in power, although he continued to cause problems for the rest of the decade. Throughout the 1990s, the United States and its allies continued to watch Iraq. They were prepared to intervene with military force if Iraq attacked its neighbor again.

New Administration

Just after the Persian Gulf War ended, Americans gave George Bush an approval rating of 91 percent, the highest ever for an American president. Yet just one year later, America had slipped into an economic recession. Bush's popularity slipped dramatically. Bush had reluctantly agreed to raise taxes, which broke his 1988 campaign pledge, "Read my lips, no new taxes." Bush fought a losing battle in the 1992 presidential election. The Democrats, with their rallying cry, "It's the economy, stupid!" blamed Republican economic policies for ruining the nation's economy. Democratic candidate Bill Clinton, the governor of Arkansas, and his running mate, Al Gore, said they were new Democrats, not the old tax and spend liberals. A third presidential candidate, Texas billionaire H. Ross Perot of the Reform party, provided lively and folksy analyses of what was wrong with the two major parties, but he won little support when the votes were counted. In the end, Clinton was elected president.

The Clinton administration proposed sweeping changes right from the start. First Lady Hillary Rodham Clinton took on the task of reforming America's health care system. Health care reform, however, did not go far, and at the end of the decade, thirty-seven million Americans were still left without health insurance.

Waco Siege

Attorney General Janet Reno faced criticism for her handling of a cult situation just over two months after entering office. On April 19, 1993, more than eighty people—members of a cult called the Branch Davidians—died after setting fire to their housing compound in Waco, Texas. Back on February 28, government agents tried to serve cult leader David Koresh with a warrant. Koresh and his followers had responded with gunshots and killed six federal agents and wounded sixteen. Six Davidians had been killed. A standoff occurred with the

A Diverse Administration

During his campaign, Bill Clinton had promised to hire women and minorities for important government positions. He fulfilled that goal. African American Ron Brown became commerce secretary, and Hispanic American Henry Cisneros became housing and urban development secretary. Janet Reno (*pictured*) became America's first woman attorney general, Donna Shalala became secretary of health and human services, African American Jocelyn Elders became surgeon general, Ruth Bader Ginsberg was appointed to the United States Supreme Court, and women headed the Council of Economic Advisers and the Environmental Protection Agency. In 1996, Clinton appointed Madeleine Albright as the nation's first woman secretary of state.

cult members refusing to surrender to federal agents. When the FBI moved to force the cult out of the compound after two months, Koresh decided to die and to take his followers with him. Many Americans blamed the FBI—and Attorney General Janet Reno—for the tragic deaths of the cult members.

After a fifty-one-day standoff with the FBI, Branch Davidians set fire to their compound in Waco.

A Second Term

In 1994, Republicans in Congress announced a ten-point Contract with America to promote the policies they stood for. In part because of numerous controversies in which the president was involved, in the 1994 elections Republicans took control of both houses of Congress for the first time since 1954. The newly elected Speaker of the House, Newt Gingrich, led the Republicans in bitter battles against Democratic policies. Republicans were particularly angry about Clinton's $280 billion tax hike, the largest tax increase in America's history.

Although the economy had grown much stronger during Clinton's first term in office, Republicans partially shut down the government twice in a battle over the federal budget. Many Americans, however, still liked Bill Clinton. Inflation was down, family income was up, and unemployment had fallen to 5.6 percent. So in 1996, Americans reelected Clinton to a second term in office.

Clinton Is Impeached

American prosperity continued during Bill Clinton's second administration, but his presidency was undermined by scandal. In 1997, lawyers heard rumors about an affair between Bill Clinton and Monica Lewinsky, a twenty-two-year-old intern at the White House. Clinton, testifying under oath in another case in which he had been accused of sexual harassment, denied having sexual relations with Lewinsky. Meanwhile, a friend of Lewinsky's named Linda Tripp secretly recorded Lewinsky's emotional account of the affair with Clinton. Tripp then gave the tape to investigator Kenneth Starr. Attorney General Janet Reno approved Starr's request to investigate Clinton's possible lying under oath.

Newspaper and television reports were filled with accounts of the alleged affair. Clinton declared on national television that he had not had a sexual affair with Monica Lewinsky. It soon became apparent that Clinton had lied. Clinton later apologized to the nation on television.

Republicans in Congress, along with some Democrats, condemned Clinton's behavior and began hearings to see if there were grounds to impeach the president, or formally accuse him of wrongdoing. Eventually, Bill Clinton was impeached on two articles—perjury and obstruction of justice. Although having a sexual affair is not a crime, lying about it in court is. He became the second United States president (Andrew Johnson was the first), and the first elected president, to be impeached. If convicted by the Senate, he would have been removed from office. The Senate vote was 55–45 against conviction on the first article, and 50–50 on the second. A two-thirds vote was needed to remove the president, so Clinton survived the ordeal.

Changes to the Soviet Union

In one of the most surprising political developments of the 1990s, the Soviet Union fell apart. For decades, America's spy agencies had grossly overestimated the strength of the Soviet economy. On August 19, 1991, Mikhail Gorbachev, the leader who had tried to reform the Soviet system, was almost overthrown by a group of political leaders who wanted to return to a strict communist form of government. Boris Yeltsin, who was president of Russia, stood up on a tank in Moscow and defied the organizers of the overthrow. Commanders of key army units refused to order their troops to fire on the demonstrators in Red Square. The coup failed, and Gorbachev was returned to power. On August 23, the government suspended all activities of the communist party. And on December 25, the Soviet Union was dissolved. All former member states of the Soviet Empire became independent. Gorbachev resigned because the Soviet Union he had governed no longer existed.

White House intern Monica Lewinsky was the focus of media attention.

President Boris Yeltsin struggled to rebuild Russia.

Throughout the rest of the decade, Russia and the other former Soviet republics struggled to reform their economies and become more democratic. Russian leader Boris Yeltsin faced huge problems. Russia's transition from a planned economy to a free market economy was marred by corruption. Currency was dangerously devalued, and life became difficult for most Russians, who wondered if they had not been better off under communism. In 1993, Yeltsin had to send troops and tanks to put down a revolt by former members of the legislature. To add to Russia's woes, in 1994 a disastrous war with separatists in Chechnya, who were struggling to secede from Russia, ended inconclusively. By decade's end, the war had resumed.

Ethnic Cleansing in Bosnia

Back in 1914, the Austrian Archduke Franz Ferdinand had been assassinated in Sarajevo, the capital of the Balkan republic of Bosnia, which set off World War I. In the 1990s, the Balkans once again became the setting for bloodshed, torture, and murder. Many of these troubles were caused by one man—the Butcher of the Balkans, Slobodan Milosevic.

When the communist regimes of Eastern Europe fell in 1990 and Russia itself abandoned communism in 1991, Yugoslavia's communist leader Milosevic, who had risen to power in the late 1980s, saw the writing on the wall. When various states of Yugoslavia—Slovenia, Croatia, Bosnia (Bosnia-Herzegovina), and Macedonia—one by one declared their independence, Milosevic found himself in charge of a much smaller Yugoslavia made up of only Serbia and Montenegro. He seized on nationalism as a force to replace communism. He planned to create a greater Serbia by extending Serb control over parts of Croatia and Bosnia. Playing upon ancient ethnic and religious hatreds, he whipped up support among the Serbs for wars of aggression against their Balkan neighbors.

In 1991, the Yugoslav Army attacked Slovenia but was quickly repelled. Milosevic then launched an attack against Croatia. Croatian strongman Franjo Tudjman put up a fierce resistance. Serbian citizens of Croatia were caught in the middle and suffered along with the Croatians.

More than elsewhere in Yugoslavia, Bosnia seemed to have achieved a true multiethnic society. Bosnian Muslims, Serbs, and Croatians had been living in peace and harmony for many years. But in 1992, Bosnian Serbs, under the leadership of Radovan Karadzic and with the strong support of Milosevic, began a campaign of ethnic cleansing. Suddenly, old friends and neighbors turned against each other. Entire populations of villages were driven out of Bosnia and, in many cases, massacred. The capital city of Sarajevo was frequently bombed by Serb forces in the surrounding hills. Much of the city was destroyed and many of its citizens killed.

By 1995, Milosevic realized that he would not succeed in reclaiming Bosnian and Croatian territory. United Nations peacekeeping forces had for the most part been unable to protect Bosnian citizens, but United Nations sanctions were causing serious problems for Yugoslavia's economy. The Serbs also faced pressure from other nations. In 1994, American jet fighters shot down four Serbian jets over Bosnia. And in 1995, the Croatian Army expelled Serbs from traditional Serb enclaves in Croatia.

Milosevic traveled to Dayton, Ohio, where, on behalf of the Bosnian Serbs, he signed a peace agreement ending the war with the Bosnian Muslims and the Croatians. American peacekeeping troops were sent to Bosnia, where they would be stationed for years to come.

Conflict in the Balkans

In 1998, a long-standing feud between the Serbs and ethnic Albanians in the southern Serbian province of Kosovo developed into an

Serbian president Slobodan Milosevic was charged with war crimes.

In Kosovo entire villages were evacuated or destroyed.

armed conflict between Serbian police forces and the Kosovo Liberation Army (KLA). The KLA sought independence from Serbia. In 1999, Slobodan Milosevic launched a full-scale military operation in Kosovo. Once again, his strategy consisted of ethnic cleansing. Entire villages were burned and their inhabitants forced out or killed.

The United States and its allies feared that the instability of Albania, Kosovo, and Macedonia could spread to surrounding countries such as Bulgaria, Greece, and Turkey. This might trigger a general war in the southern Balkans. To stop Serbian aggression, the United States and its allies began air strikes over Kosovo and Serbia in March 1999. Nine hundred targets, including the Yugoslavian capital city, Belgrade, were bombed. By June, there had been a total of thirty-two thousand bomber missions. Serbian forces had been driven out of Kosovo, and the war ended.

The Kosovo Liberation Army's ethnic Albanians wanted to be independent from Serbia. Their campaign resulted in Milosovec's campaign of ehtnic cleansing.

Rwandan Genocide

Ethnic differences were at the root of many of the wars that erupted in Africa during the 1990s. By far the worst episode of ethnic violence occurred in 1994 in the nation of Rwanda, a small country in the center of Africa. Rwanda's population is divided between two ethnic groups: the majority Hutu, who made up 80 percent of the population, and the minority Tutsi, who nonetheless dominated the Hutus economically. Historically, there were many clashes between members of these two groups.

In 1990, a Tutsi rebel group began fighting Rwanda's government. That conflict appeared to be settled in 1993, when Rwanda's Hutu president agreed to share power with the Tutsis. In April 1994, however, the president was killed when his plane was shot down. Immediately afterward, Hutu government officials organized and began a policy of genocide against the Tutsi. The Hutu-dominated army went on a two-month rampage butchering more than eight hundred thousand Tutsi people.

The genocide finally ended in July, when the Tutsi rebels took the capital city of Kigali and the Rwandan government fled. United Nations peacekeeping troops were in Rwanda when the genocides took place, but the UN failed to give the peacekeepers authority to use force to stop the killing.

An End to Apartheid

The 1990s brought remarkable political progress to South Africa. For most of the twentieth century, South Africa's white minority had ruled the country. Since 1948, the government used an unfair system of laws called apartheid to discriminate against blacks. South Africans were separated into three groups: whites, blacks, and colored, or people of mixed descent. Apartheid gave whites every advantage. They lived in the best neighborhoods, earned

Ethnic conflict in Rwanda resulted in wars and genocide.

South Africa's longstanding policy of apartheid finally came to an end.

more money at work, and received better educations. Meanwhile, nonwhites lived in poverty and labored under harsh rules.

From the beginning, black South Africans opposed apartheid. At first, they staged peaceful protests and strikes. In 1960, the struggle against apartheid turned deadly. A large crowd gathered in the town of Sharpeville to protest apartheid surrounded the police station and threw rocks. In response, the white police officers opened fire. They continued shooting even after the protesters began running away. Sixty-nine people were killed, and one hundred eighty more were injured in the Sharpeville massacre.

The Sharpeville massacre was a turning point in South African history. Black groups began using violence to end apartheid. Other countries began criticizing South Africa's unfair laws. For decades, the white government rejected all calls to change apartheid. Instead, it cracked down on black political groups by throwing leaders in jail.

During the 1980s, as riots erupted on South African streets, the United States and many other countries imposed trade restrictions in an attempt to end apartheid. Rock stars and other famous figures spoke out against the policy.

In 1990, South African President F. W. de Klerk took the first steps toward ending the country's isolation. In February, he freed Nelson Mandela, the heroic freedom fighter who had been in prison for twenty-seven years. He also legalized the African National Congress (ANC), which had been fighting against the apartheid policy of South Africa's white rulers for decades. More progress quickly followed as the government began to repeal the nation's apartheid laws.

In 1992, white South Africans voted to end rule by the minority whites by 1994. In 1993, de Klerk and Mandela shared the Nobel Peace Prize. And in 1994, in South Africa's first fully free elections,

Mandela became the nation's new president, and de Klerk became vice president. In 1996, South African lawmakers passed a new democratic constitution, which guaranteed equal rights for all citizens, although the nation continues to face economic and political problems caused by the transition.

Bombing of US Embassies in Africa

In 1998, the terrorist organization al-Qaeda staged a pair of deadly attacks against American targets. Two US embassies in Africa were bombed.

At almost the exact same time on August 7, 1998, al-Qaeda attacked the US embassies in Kenya and Tanzania. Powerful blasts rocked both buildings. The Kenya bomb killed 213 people, including 12 Americans. The rest were Kenyans who worked in and around the embassy. Eleven people died in the Tanzania blast. Both explosions injured many innocent bystanders.

President Bill Clinton wanted to punish al-Qaeda for the embassy attacks, yet he did not wish to risk the lives of US soldiers. He decided to strike al-Qaeda camps with cruise missiles. The unmanned missiles hit targets in Sudan and Afghanistan. They did little meaningful damage, however.

Middle East Peace Talks

For true peace to prevail in the war-weary Middle East, Israel and the Palestinians would have to come to terms agreeable to both sides. The territory controlled by Israel is of great religious importance to the parties involved—the Jews of Israel and the Muslim Palestinians and Arabs. Those who wanted peace in the region were encouraged by developments in 1993. President Bill Clinton hosted peace talks in Washington, D.C., between Israeli leader Yitzhak Rabin and Palestinian Liberation Organization (PLO) leader Yasser Arafat. The

Nelson Mandela

Black activist Nelson Mandela devoted his life to ending apartheid. Mandela was born in Umtata, South Africa, in 1918. As a young lawyer, he helped lead the African National Congress, a group opposed to apartheid. Because he opposed the white government, in 1964 Mandela was sentenced to life in prison. Nelson Mandela became a worldwide symbol of the injustice of apartheid. Foreign governments demanded his release. In 1990, President F. W. de Klerk freed Mandela. The two worked together to end apartheid peacefully. They received the Nobel Peace Prize in 1993. A year later, Nelson Mandela became South Africa's first black president. He spent his later years ailing but very much involved in activism and philanthropy. Nelson Mandela died in 2013 at the age of 95.

PLO leader Yasser Arafat signed a peace accord with Israel.

two signed peace accords and outlined areas of agreement and a timeline of issues that needed to be negotiated before the signing of a final peace agreement. Among the provisions of the accord was a plan for Israel to withdraw from the Gaza Strip and the West Bank, which the Palestinians would be able to govern themselves.

Sadly, in 1995, Rabin was assassinated by a Jewish religious fanatic. His tragic death showed how difficult it was to achieve peace in a region where many people on both sides have strong feelings against peace. By the end of the decade, the peace process had made some slow progress. Palestinians controlled most of the land in the West Bank and the Gaza Strip, which was designated to become the new Palestinian state. The most difficult issue left to be decided was the future status of Jerusalem—a city both sides claimed as their capital. The area remained politically tense through the end of the century, with riots and bloodshed continuing to occur.

HIV/AIDS Ravages Africa

During the 1990s, HIV/AIDS became a major health crisis in Africa. It still ravages Africa today. Because HIV compromises a body's immune system, AIDS patients often suffer from many illnesses. Over time, these illnesses combine to weaken the patient, who usually dies. There are three ways that a person can get HIV. One way is through contact with infected blood—for example, by sharing a contaminated hypodermic needle. Another way is by having sex with an infected partner. Lastly, an infected mother may pass the virus on to her baby.

HIV/AIDS has affected nearly every nation in the world. The disease strikes hardest in poor countries. Their governments are weak and face many other problems. Health care is limited. People have little education and may not know how to avoid infection. The disease thrives in these conditions. About 95 percent of all HIV-infected people live in poor countries.

Africa quickly became the center of the HIV/AIDS epidemic. The continent has long struggled with poverty, war, and corruption. In the 1990s, the disease spread out of control in Africa. Many African governments were slow to teach their citizens how to protect themselves from HIV. The virus spread rapidly. Infected women often gave birth to infected babies.

Today, African governments are working hard to slow the spread of the virus. Nations from around the globe are helping them. Yet progress is slow. Roughly seven thousand new infections occur each day in Africa. Seven out of every ten HIV/AIDS victims come from that continent. The virus has helped shorten the average life span in Africa. In several African nations, the average person now dies around age 40.

As young adults grow ill and die from the disease, Africa's problems worsen. More children are becoming orphans. Some regions face a shortage of workers. There are not enough farmers to grow food. Schools have too few teachers. The effects of HIV/AIDS will continue to be felt in Africa for decades to come.

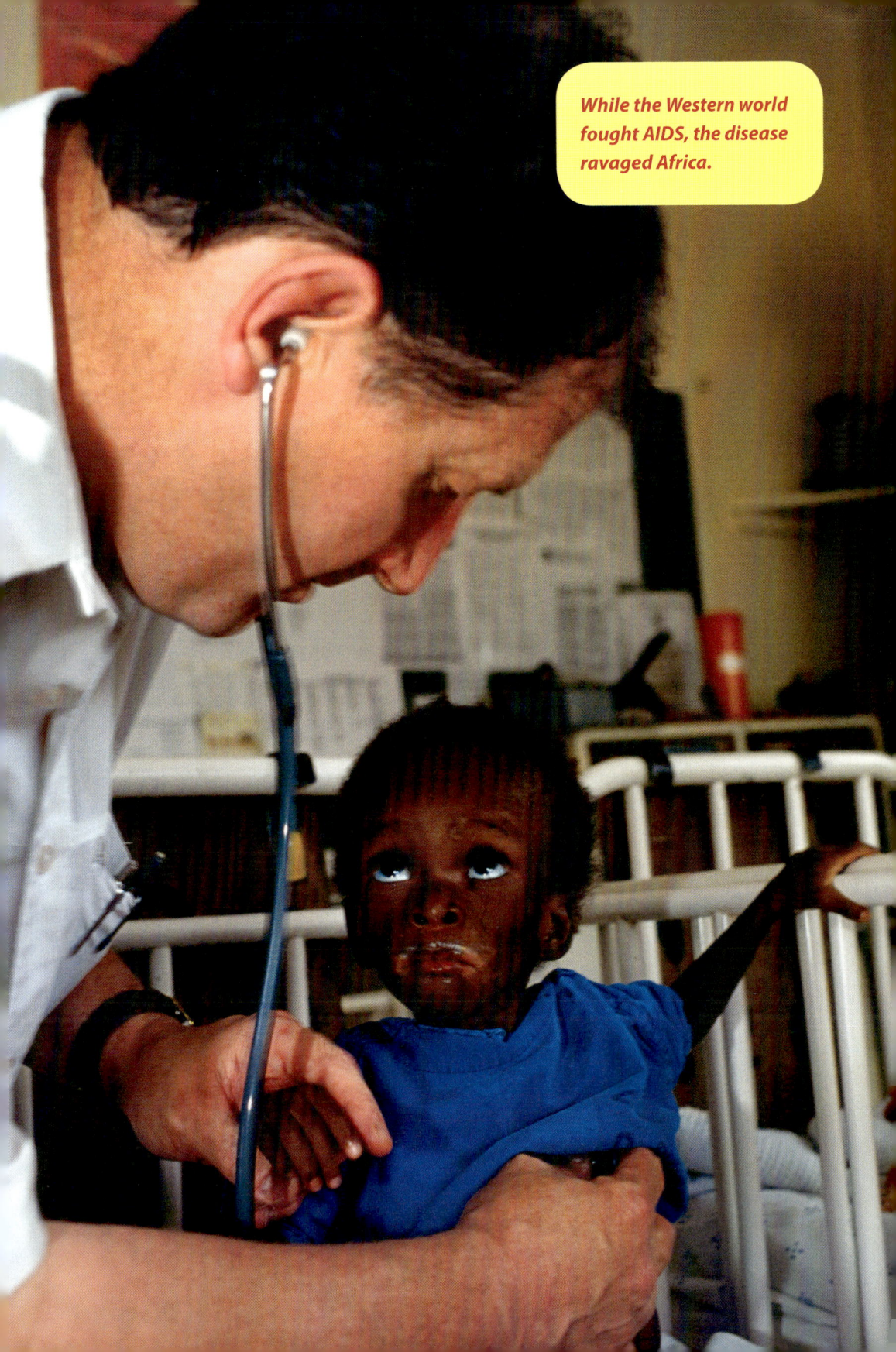
While the Western world fought AIDS, the disease ravaged Africa.

Advances in Science, Technology, and Medicine

As the year 2000, also known as Y2K, approached, doomsayers of all sorts—from religious fanatics to people afraid of technology—began to predict the coming end of the world—or at least the collapse of civilization.

Getting Ready for Y2K

By the end of the 1990s, the entire world was computerized. Many governments and other vital businesses could no longer function without computers. Unfortunately, computer programs written several decades earlier could not distinguish any year beyond 1999. The next date after December 31, 1999, that the computer could recognize would be January 1, 1900. Programmers had assumed that the defect would be corrected long before it became a problem.

According to the doomsday scenario, planes would fall from the sky (so few people scheduled flights on New Year's Eve), financial systems would collapse (so people were told to withdraw money from the bank and have cash on hand), and distribution systems would break down (so people were told to stock up on food and other supplies). Even scarier was the possibility that missiles armed with nuclear warheads might be automatically launched by computer error.

The world held its breath as New Year's Eve approached. In spite of widespread apprehension, spectacular New Year's extravaganzas with elaborate fireworks displays went off without a hitch in many of the world's major cities. The Y2K disaster never happened. Financial institutions, major corporations, and government agencies had begun converting their computer systems several years earlier. They were well prepared for the coming of Y2K.

Discovering Other Galaxies

In the 1990s, astronomers learned that there are other solar systems—stars far out in space that have planets orbiting around them just like our sun. Of course, nobody has actually seen these planets because they are too far away. But unmistakable evidence for their existence has been discovered.

What the astronomers saw was a slight wobble in the movement of a star known as Upsilon Andromedae. Located forty-four light years from Earth in the Milky Way galaxy, it is believed to have three huge Jupiter-like planets spinning around it. The planets' gravity tugs on the star, causing it to wobble.

Since the Milky Way galaxy contains more than two hundred billion stars, scientists estimate that there could be many billions of planets. To determine if there are other civilizations in the universe, a scientific effort known as the Search for Extraterrestrial Intelligence, or SETI, has been scanning the heavens. Some teams have used radio telescopes to look and listen for radio signals among the billions of radio frequencies flooding the universe. Other teams have used optical telescopes to look for signals in pulses of light from the stars.

An Asteroid Could Mean the End

In 1980, physicist Luis Alvarez and his son Walter theorized that an asteroid or comet crashed into Earth about sixty-five million years

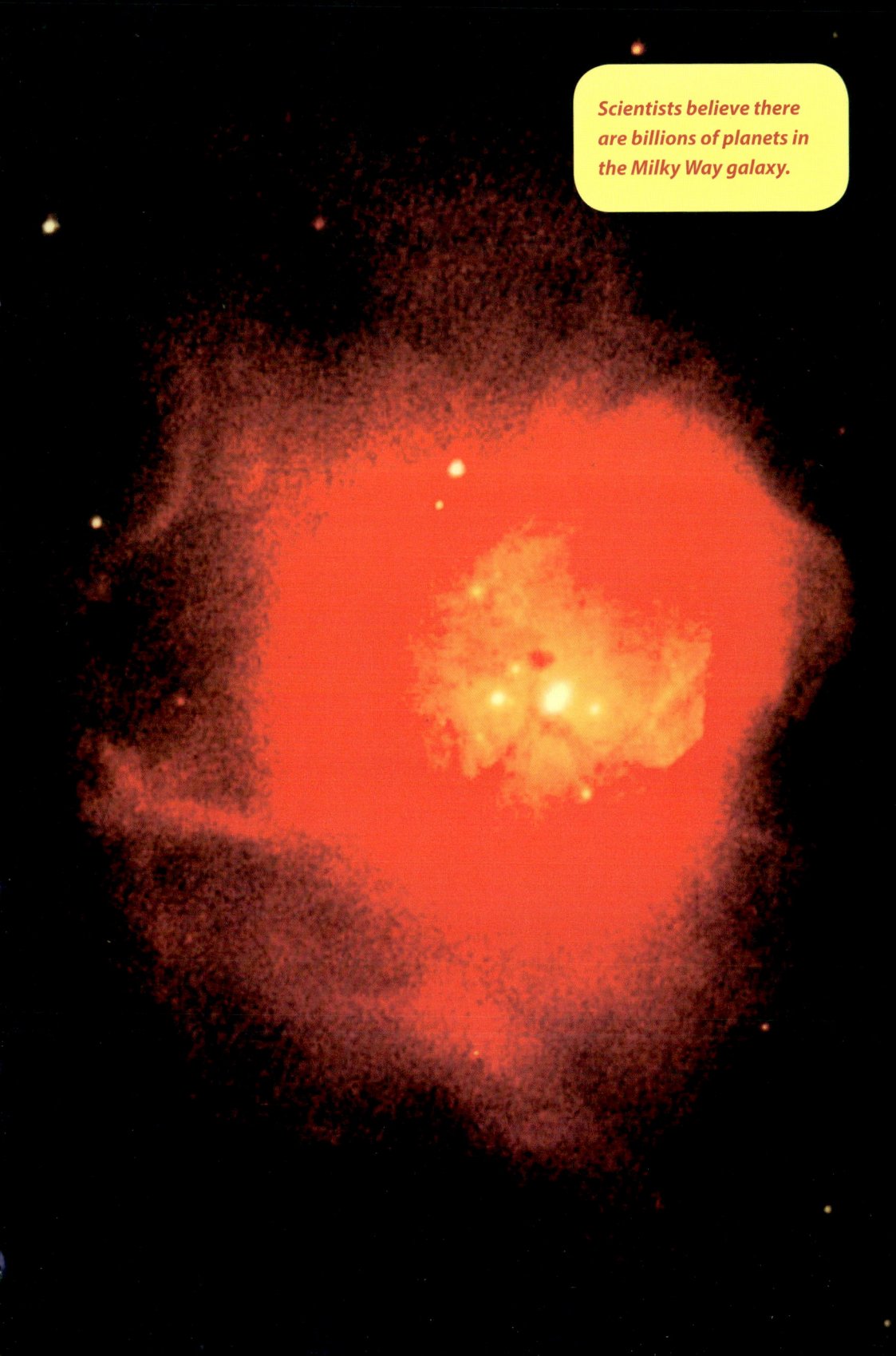

Scientists believe there are billions of planets in the Milky Way galaxy.

Scientists debated humans' impact on climate change.

ago. They had discovered a layer of iridium in the ground, a rare element that later was found to extend around the world. The Alvarezes proposed that the iridium had been delivered to earth by an asteroid. The asteroid's impact produced huge clouds of dust that hid the sun for several years, causing a mass extinction of many forms of life including the dinosaurs. In 1991, scientists pinpointed the site of the impact as the Chicxulub crater in the Yucatan in Mexico. Evidence at the site indicates that the asteroid must have been six to nine miles (10 to 15 km) in diameter, and it must have hit earth at a speed of 93,000 miles per hour (150,000 km/h).

Scientists believe that other previous mass extinctions in earth's history may also have been caused by asteroid or comet impacts. They also believe earth will again be struck by a killer asteroid sometime in the future. And in July 1994, as if to demonstrate the potential danger to earth lurking in the depths of space, astronomers witnessed the spectacular impact of the Shoemaker-Levy 9 comet into the planet Jupiter. This was the first time human beings witnessed a comet crashing into a planet. The awesome event on Jupiter served as a wake-up call to astronomers, who called for renewed efforts to find all the objects in space that could someday threaten earth.

Climate Change

Although the issue is still widely debated , most scientists now believe that the world is, indeed, growing warmer. The 1990s were the warmest decade on record, and 1998 was the warmest year ever recorded. Huge sections of the Antarctic ice shelf broke off and began drifting in the surrounding ocean. At the North Pole, areas usually covered by ice all year long are now melting to become free of ice during the summer.

If steps are not taken to stop the warming trend, many scientists believe that sometime in the twenty-first century, the sea level may rise.

Exploring Space

Technology in the 1990s made it possible to study space like never before. The Hubble Space Telescope revealed distant secrets of the universe. Meanwhile, the *Mars Pathfinder* probed the surface of another planet. These two machines led scientists to amazing new discoveries.

Unlike other telescopes, Hubble orbits earth from outside the atmosphere, which enables a much clearer view of the universe than ground-based telescopes. Launched in 1990, Hubble has recorded brilliant images of distant stars and planets. Thanks to the Hubble Space Telescope, scientists now believe that there are about 125 billion galaxies in the universe.

The *Mars Pathfinder* landed on Mars on July 4, 1997, and beamed back stunning pictures of the Martian landscape. *Pathfinder* then released a small six-wheeled remote-controlled vehicle called *Sojourner*. Scientists on earth used the rover to study Martian rocks and soil. For three months, *Pathfinder* and *Sojourner* sent back valuable data about Mars. Their mission ended in October 1997 when their batteries finally died.

Coastal cities around the globe, where most of the world's population lives, will be hit hard by flooding and other related disasters.

Human Genome Project

In December 1999, researchers involved in the publicly funded effort Human Genome Project announced that they had traced the chemical sequence of chromosome 22, one of the twenty-three sets of molecules that provide the genetic map for human life. Francis Collins, the scientist who headed the project, said, "This is the first time that we've had a complete chapter in the human instruction book." Collins's researchers discovered the order of about 545 of the estimated 700 genes on chromosome 22, or about 1.1 percent of the genes in the human body. The scientists could not have even begun the project without the aid of powerful supercomputers.

Scientists expect that the genome project will eventually be able to give doctors the unprecedented ability to use gene therapy to cure diseases. Once they understand the differences in each individual's genetic makeup, they will be able to custom design drugs targeted for specific individuals.

A Sheep Is Cloned

One of the most fascinating developments of the twentieth century took place in 1997, when Scottish scientist Dr. Ian Wilmut successfully created a cloned sheep. Taking a single cell from an adult sheep, Wilmut was able to create a baby lamb that was a clone. In other words, it had the exact same genetic information as the adult sheep. Wilmut named the clone Dolly.

Wilmut's clone opened new worlds of possibility for genetic science. Some people were thrilled with the advancement and saw it as a way to prevent endangered animals from becoming extinct. Scientists have since cloned other animals, such as cows, pigs, and rabbits.

However, the clones are not as healthy as the original animals. Others saw cloning as a dangerous new tool. Although human cloning is not yet possible, scientists believe it will be in the future. Most people are opposed to the idea of ever cloning a human. They warn about the dangers of meddling with nature.

Nanotechnology

Nanotechnology, the science of the tiny, emerged during the 1990s. This revolutionary technology involves the manipulation of matter at the atomic or molecular level. The main unit of measure, the nanometer, is the width of three atoms. Scientists hope to someday build tiny devices, atom by atom, for use in miniaturized manufacturing, drug-delivery systems, and nanocomputers. Researchers have discovered new types of carbon molecules called fullerenes. In May 1998, Richard E. Smalley and his colleagues at the Center for Nanoscale Science and Technology at Rice University in Houston, Texas, used fullerenes to create thin tubes with closed ends called nanotubes. The nanotubes were one hundred times stronger than steel, yet six times lighter. By the end of the decade, many organizations in the United States, Europe, and Japan were conducting research in nanotechnology.

Revival of the Electric Car

Electric cars rely on electricity rather than petroleum. While the electric car dates back to the nineteenth century, gasoline-driven cars have historically been preferred due to their affordability and performance. The energy crisis of the 1970s sparked a revival of interest in the electric car. So did concerns about the environment. American auto manufacturers were driven to develop modern electric cars, but very few people purchased them.

In 1990, an amendment to the Clean Air Act asked automakers to develop cleaner cars with lower fuel emissions. They responded with several models that did not take off. Eventually, better models emerged, as did hybrid models that began to catch on—particularly when the economy took a downturn and gasoline became prohibitively expensive. Electric cars and hybrids are more expensive than gasoline-powered automobiles, and that may explain their lack of popularity.

Conclusion

The 1990s were a decade of great change. Americans had reason to be optimistic about the future. With the end of the Cold War, nuclear war no longer loomed as a likely threat. But the world was still dangerous. Americans learned that they still had much to fear from terrorists at home, as well as abroad. In addition, too great a dependence on foreign oil meant that events in the troubled Middle East could cause serious economic problems for America.

The 1990s were a prosperous period for most Americans. The economy during the two administrations of President Bill Clinton grew healthier each year. Unemployment fell to low levels, as did inflation. Even so, there was still much work to be done to make sure that all Americans regardless of race or sex had equal access to education and job opportunities.

Still, there were many positive happenings during the decade. Amazing advances in medical science were made, such as a more profound understanding of the human genome. Such breakthroughs promised that in the coming century Americans would live longer, healthier, and potentially happier lives.

As clocks ticked toward midnight on December 31, 1999, the anticipation grew. All over the world, people gathered with friends, neighbors, or crowds of complete strangers to welcome the start of a new millennium. In cities and towns on every continent, huge celebrations marked the occasion.

The joyful mood would not last very long. Old problems do not go away simply because the calendar changes. For years, American politics had been bitterly divided between Democrats and Republicans

Bill Clinton led the United States for most of the decade.

and liberals and conservatives. That bitterness would reach new levels during the presidential election of 2000. The election was one of the most controversial in US history, and it would only be decided by one of the most deabted Supreme Court decisions in history.

The new president, George W. Bush, soon faced a severe test. On September 11, 2001, al-Qaeda terrorists killed nearly three thousand Americans with hijacked airplanes. The president responded by ordering an invasion of Afghanistan, whose government was sheltering al-Qaeda members. The Bush administration also used the September 11 attacks to justify an invasion of Iraq in 2003. Eventually, that decision would prove very unpopular. But it was just one of the reasons the American people grew angry with the Republican president and the Republicans in Congress who supported his policies.

Democrats did very well in the 2008 elections. They picked up seats in the Senate and House of Representatives. Most notably, however, a Democrat who promised change won the presidency and made history. As the first decade of the new millennium came to a close, the United States was led by Barack Obama—the nation's first African American president.

Timeline

1990 The Human Genome Project begins. On February 11, Nelson Mandela is freed from prison in South Africa. On August 2, Iraq invades Kuwait, which will lead to the Persian Gulf War.

1991 On January 16, the United States and its allies begin a bombing campaign against Iraq, which marks the start of the Persian Gulf War (led in part by Norman Schwarzkopf). On February 23, a ground invasion begins against Iraq. Within one hundred hours, Saddam Hussein agrees to a cease-fire. On August 19, communist hardliners try to oust Soviet leader Mikhail Gorbachev, but the coup is put down in part through the efforts of Russian President Boris Yeltsin. On December 25, the Soviet Union is dissolved. Rodney King is arrested and beaten by police in Los Angeles. Tiger Woods becomes the youngest winner of the United States Junior Amateur championship. Basketball star Magic Johnson reveals that he has HIV/AIDS. The Yugloslav Army launches an attack against Croatia.

1992 On April 29, riots break out in Los Angeles after the police officers accused of beating Rodney King are acquitted. On November 3, Bill Clinton is elected president. Bosnian Serbs begin campaign of ethnic cleansing. White South Africans vote to end rule by whites by 1994.

1993 On February 26, Muslim terrorists bomb the World Trade Center in New York City. On February 28, a violent clash takes place between federal agents and members of the Branch Davidian cult in Waco, Texas. On April 19, the Branch Davidians die when they set fire to their housing compound. On September 13, Israeli leader Yitzhak Rabin and Palestinian leader Yasir  Arafat sign historic peace accords in Washington, D.C. On October 4, Russian President Boris Yeltsin's troops put down a revolt by former legislators. Nelson Mandela and South African President F. W. de Klerk share the Nobel Peace Prize. Steven Spielberg releases *Jurassic Park* and *Schindler's List*. Tennis champion Arthur Ashe dies from HIV/AIDS.

1994 On April 29, South Africa holds its first free elections, in which Nelson Mandela is elected president. In June, Nicole Brown Simpson and Ron Goldman are murdered, starting the O. J. Simpson murder case. In August, major-league baseball players go on strike. On November 8, Republicans win control of both houses of Congress and announce sweeping legislation called the Contract With America. On December 11, Russia begins a war with separatists in Chechnya. Hutu officials in Rwanda organize a massive genocidal attack on the Tutsi people. Musician Kurt Cobain commits suicide. In August, a twenty-fifth anniversary Woodstock concert is held in New York State. The sitcom *Friends* debuts on television.

1995 On April 19, Timothy McVeigh bombs the Alfred P. Murrah Building in Oklahoma City. On October 3, O. J. Simpson is found not guilty of murdering his ex-wife Nicole Brown Simpson and Ron Goldman. On November 4, Israeli leader Yitzhak Rabin is assassinated. On December 14, a treaty is signed to end war in Bosnia.

1996 Scottish scientists clone a sheep, which they name Dolly. On April 3, police arrest Theodore Kaczynski, the suspected Unabomber. On November 5, Bill Clinton is reelected president. On December 12, Madeleine Albright becomes the first woman secretary of state.

1997 In July, *Pathfinder* lands on the surface of Mars. Tiger Woods becomes the first African American to win the Masters Tournament. On August 31, Princess Diana is killed in an

Timeline **89**

automobile accident. President Bill Clinton's affair with White House intern Monica Lewinsky comes to light. *Titanic* premieres in theaters.

1998 On January 22, Theodore Kaczynski pleads guilty. In June, armed conflict breaks out in Kosovo. Mark McGwire and Sammy Sosa break Roger Maris's 1961 record of 61 home runs in a season. On December 19, Bill Clinton is impeached by the House of Representatives.

1999 On February 12, the Senate acquits Bill Clinton. In March, the United States and allied troops start an air war over Kosovo and Serbia, which brings an end to the fighting there by June. On April 20, two high school students kill twelve other students, a teacher, and themselves at Columbine High School in Littleton, Colorado. In December, researchers announce completion of the Human Genome Project. On December 31, Y2K fears prove unjustified.

90 The 1990s

Glossary

al-Qaeda—A terrorist group responsible for many attacks, including 9/11.

apartheid—A policy of racial separation and discrimination against blacks in South Africa that ended in the 1990s.

clone—In science, to create an exact copy of a plant or animal.

coalition—A temporary alliance of people or nations.

epidemic—The widespread outbreak of a disease.

ethnic—Referring to a group's race, religion, or culture.

genocide—The planned destruction of an ethnic group.

HIV/AIDS—A disease that weakens the body's ability to fight off other diseases.

human genome project—An international research effort to determine the DNA sequence of the entire human genome.

impeach—A process in which a public official is formally accused of misconduct.

massacre—The act of killing a large number of people.

network—A system of computers connected to share data.

perjury—The act of falsifying information or telling untruths in court after being sworn in.

rampage—A series of violent and frenzied actions.

refugee—A person who flees to find safety from a war or other disaster.

sitcom—Short for situational comedy; it is a type of television show.

terrorism—The use of violence and fear to achieve political goals.

Further Reading

Books

Cruden, Alexander. *The Persian Gulf War*. Farmington Hills, Mich.: Greenhaven Press, 2011.

Dakers, Diane. *Nelson Mandela*. New York, N.Y.: Crabtree Publishing Company, 2014.

Gerdes, Louise, editor. *The Columbine High School Shooting*. Farmington Hills, Mich: Greenhaven Press, 2012.

Nardo, Don. *The Rwandan Genocide*. Detroit, Mich.: Lucent Books, 2011.

Nelson, Michael and Barbara Perry, editors. *41: Inside the Presidency of George H.W. Bush*. Ithaca, N.Y.: Cornell University Press, 2014.

Takiff, Michael. *A Complicated Man: The Life of Bill Clinton as Told by Those Who Knew Him*. New Haven, Conn.: Yale University Press, 2011.

Web Sites

pbs.org/wgbh/pages/frontline/gulf/
The companion Web site to Frontline's analysis of the Gulf War.

pbs.org/wgbh/pages/frontline/shows/mandela/
The companion website to Frontline's program on Nelson Mandela.

whitehouse.gov/history/presidents/bc42.html
The official White House fact sheet for President Bill Clinton.

Movies

Hotel Rwanda. Directed by Terry George. Santa Monica, Calif.: Lions Gate Entertainment, 2004.

A true story of a man who saved refugees from the Rwandan genocide.

Mandela: Long Walk to Freedom. Directed by Justin Chadwick. Los Angeles, Calif.: 20th Century Fox, 2013.

A biopic about Nelson Mandela.

Titanic. Directed by James Cameron. Los Angeles, Calif.: 20th Century Fox, 1997.

Hugely popular movie of the 1990s; a love story set on the sinking ship.

Index

A

Advanced Research Projects Agency Network (ARPANET), 14
African National Congress (ANC), 67, 69
Aguilera, Christina, 33
al-Qaeda, 8, 15, 17, 68, 86
Albania, 63
Albright, Madeleine, 53
Alfred P. Murrah Building, 17
Alvarez, Luis and Walter, 76, 79
Amazon.com, 11, 12
American Pearl, 47
Anthony, Marc, 33
apartheid, 64, 67, 69
Arafat, Yasser, 68
Ashe, Arthur, 44
Asteroids, 76, 79

B

Baltimore Orioles, 42
baseball, 41, 42
Beanie Babies, 25
Berlin Wall, 7
Berners-Lee, Timothy, 14
Bezos, Jeff, 11
Blades, Rubén, 33
Bosnia, 8, 59, 60
Boyz II Men, 28
Branch Davidians, 52
Bronfman, Edgar Jr., 33
Brown, Ron, 53
Buena Vista Social Club, 33
Bug's Life, A, 37
Bulgaria, 63
Bush, George, 48, 51, 52, 86

C

Cabbage Patch Kids, 25
cellular phones, 15
Chechnya, 59
Chicago Cubs, 42
Chicxulub crater, 79
Cisneros, Henry, 53
Clinton, Bill, 48, 52, 53, 55, 56, 68, 84
Clinton, Hillary Rodham, 52
cloning, 7, 8, 81, 82
Cobain, Kurt, 30, 31
Cold War, 7, 84
Collins, Francis, 81
Columbine school shooting, 8, 17, 19
communism, 7, 56, 59
Contract With America, 55
Cooder, Ry, 33
Croatia, 59, 60

D

de Klerk, F. W., 67, 68, 69
digital versatile or video disk (DVD), 36

E

eBay, 12
Elders, Jocelyn, 53
e-mail, 7, 11
ethnic cleansing, 59, 63

F

fashion, 22
Federal Bureau of Investigation (FBI), 54
Ferrer, Ibrahim, 33
Friends, 37, 38
fullerenes, 82
Furby, 25

G

gangsta rap, 28, 31
Gaza Strip, 71
Gehrig, Lou, 42
Ginsburg, Ruth Bader, 53
Goldman, Ron, 21, 22
golf, 41, 42
Gorbachev, Mikhail, 56
Gore, Al, 52
Greece, 63
grunge, 22, 30, 31, 46

H

Harris, Eric, 17, 19
Harry Potter, 34
Hitler, Adolf, 48
HIV/AIDS, 8, 44, 71, 72
Holocaust, 37
Human Genome Project, 8, 81
Hussein, Saddam, 48, 51
Hutu, 64

I

impeachment, 56
information superhighway, 9, 14
Internet, 7, 9, 11, 12, 14, 15, 30, 33
Iraq, 8, 48, 51
Israel, 68

J

Jewel, Richard, 45
Johnson, Andrew, 56
Johnson, Magic, 44
Jurassic Park, 34

K

Kaczynski, Theodore, 18
Kenya, 68
King, Rodney, 19, 21
Klebold, Dylan, 17, 19
Koresh, David, 52, 54
Kosovo, 60, 63
Kosovo Liberation Army (KLA), 63
Kuwait, 8, 48, 51

L

Lewinsky, Monica, 55
Littleton, Colorado, 17. *See also* Columbine school shooting.
Los Angeles riots, 19, 21
Louganis, Greg, 44

M

Macedonia, 59, 63
Mandela, Nelson, 67, 68, 69
Maris, Roger, 42
Martin, Ricky, 33
Masters Tournament, 42
McGwire, Mark, 42
McVeigh, Timothy, 17
Milky Way galaxy, 76
Milosevic, Slobodan, 59, 63
Montenegro, 59
Murden, Tori, 45, 47

N

nanotechnology, 82
Napster, 30
Nirvana, 30, 31
'N Sync, 28

O

Oklahoma City bombing, 8, 17, 45
Operation Desert Shield, 51
Operation Desert Storm, 51

P

Palestine Liberation Organization (PLO), 68
Perot, H. Ross, 52
Persian Gulf War, 48, 52
pet rock, 22
Powell, Colin, 51
Priceline.com, 12
Prince Charles of Wales, 25–26
Princess Diana of Wales, 25–26
Professional Golf Association (PGA), 41, 42

R

Rabin, Yitzhak, 68, 71
Reno, Janet, 52, 53, 55
Ripken, Cal, Jr., 42
Rolling Stones, 28
Rowling, J.K., 34
Russia, 7, 56, 59
Rwanda, 8, 64

S

St. Louis Cardinals, 42
Saudi Arabia, 48, 51
Saving Private Ryan, 37
Schindler, Oskar, 37
Schindler's List, 37
Schwarzkopf, Norman, 51
Search for Extraterrestrial Intelligence (SETI), 76
Seinfeld, 37, 38
Serbia, 59, 63
Shalala, Donna, 53
Simpson, Nicole Brown, 21, 22
Simpson, O. J., 21, 22
Simpsons, The, 37, 38
sitcom, 37, 38
Slovenia, 59
Sosa, Sammy, 42
Soundgarden, 31
South Africa, 64, 67, 68, 69
Soviet Union, 7, 56
Spielberg, Steven, 34, 37
Starr, Kenneth, 55
Sting, 28
Summer Olympics, 45

T

Tanzania, 68
terrorism, 8, 15, 17, 68, 84
Titanic, 37
TiVo, 36
Toy Story, 34
Trench Coat Mafia, 19
Tripp, Linda, 55
Tudjman, Franjo, 60
Turkey, 63
Tutsi, 64

U

Unabomber, 18
United Nations, 60, 64
Upsilon Andromedae, 76

W

Waco, Texas, 52
Webmasters, 12
West Bank, 71
Wilmut, Ian, 81
Woods, Eldrick "Tiger", 41, 42
World Series, 42
World Trade Center bombing, 15
World War I, 59
World War II, 7, 37
World Wide Web, 9, 14

X

X Games, 46

Y

Yeltsin, Boris, 56, 59
Y2K, 7, 75, 76
Yugoslavia, 59, 60